MW00975518

To Isaac.
May all your Christmas
wishes come true!
Love .... Aunt Meg + Uncle Mike

Isaac is ~excited~
Christmastime is here!

He says, "I wish for lots and lots
of fluffy snow this year!"

Isaac writes to Santa.
The letter takes him ages.

"Perhaps I've wished for way too much?"
(There are over 50 pages!)

Dear Santa,

Isaac decorates the tree
with twinkly lights that glow.

Christmas
decorations

Look at Isaac up on stage.
He's in the Christmas play.

He wished to make
his family proud,
and have the greatest day!

The kitchen's very busy.
Isaac smells cookies baking.

"I wish that I could eat that bowl of cookie dough Dad's making."

Isaac wakes at 5 a.m.
"It's Christmas Day!
Yippee!"

He runs downstairs to find a pile of presents beneath the tree.

This sweater's really **itchy**.
He tries to grin and bear it,
but Isaac really wishes that
he didn't have to wear it!

Isaac dresses warmly.
His wish for snow came true!

He's off to build a snowman now.
Perhaps he will build two!

Isaac's sledding down the hill,
"I wish I could *speed* up!"

His wish comes true,
his sled is = *fast*
when powered by a pup!

It's after Christmas dinner,
and everyone is snoring.
Isaac says to his best friend,
"I wish it was less **BORING!**"

Mom is asking Isaac,
"Did your **BIGGEST** wish come true?"
"Oh yes," he smiles,
"that wish was being..."

"...here with **all** of you!"

Do you wish for fun with friends,
or a family trip that never ends?
Whatever it is that you hold dear,
keep your Christmas wishes here!

I wish...

Copyright © 2018 by Sourcebooks
Sourcebooks and the colophon are
registered trademarks
of Sourcebooks, Inc.
Put Me In The Story is a
registered trademark of Sourcebooks, Inc.
All rights reserved.

Published by Put Me In The Story,
a publication of Sourcebooks, Inc.
P.O. Box 4410, Naperville, Illinois 60567-4410
(630) 961-3900
Fax: (630) 961-2168
w.putmeinthestory.com

Date of Production: August 2018
Run Number: HTW_PO201829
Printed and bound in China (GD)
10 9 8 7 6 5 4 3 2 1

put me
in the story®
Bestselling books starring your child!
www.putmeinthestory.com